ILL SEEN ILL SAID

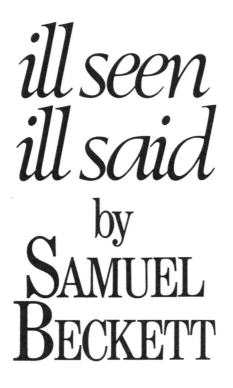

ill seen ill said

by

SAMUEL BECKETT

Translated from French by the author

Grove Press, Inc., New York

First published in French as *Mal vu mal dit*
by Les Editions de Minuit, Paris, France, 1981.

First Hardcover Edition 1981
First Printing 1981
ISBN: 0-394-52233-8
Library of Congress Catalog Card Number 81-47695

Manufactured in the United States of America

GROVE PRESS, INC., 196 West Houston Street,
New York, N.Y. 10014

ILL SEEN ILL SAID

From where she lies she sees Venus rise. On. From where she lies when the skies are clear she sees Venus rise followed by the sun. Then she rails at the source of all life. On. At evening when the skies are clear she savours its star's revenge. At the other window. Rigid upright on her old chair she watches for the radiant one. Her old deal spindlebacked kitchen chair. It emerges from out the last rays and sinking ever brighter is engulfed in its turn. On. She sits on erect and rigid in the deepening gloom. Such helplessness to move she cannot help. Heading on foot for a particular point often she freezes on the way. Unable till long after to move on not knowing whither or for what purpose. Down on her knees especially she finds it hard not to remain so forever. Hand resting on hand on some convenient support. Such as the foot of her bed. And on them her head. There then she sits as though turned to stone face to the night. Save for the white of her hair and faintly bluish white of face and hands all is black. For an eye having no need of light to see. All this in the present as had she the misfortune to be still of this world.

The cabin. Its situation. Careful. On. At the inexistent centre of a formless place. Rather more circular than otherwise finally. Flat to be sure. To cross it in a straight line takes her from five to ten minutes. Depending on her speed and radius taken. Here she who loves to—here she who now can only stray never strays. Stones increasingly abound. Ever scanter even the rankest weed. Meagre pastures hem it round on which it slowly gains. With none to gainsay. To have gainsaid. As if doomed to spread. How come a cabin in such a place? How came? Careful. Before replying that in the far past at the time of its building there was clover growing to its very walls. Implying furthermore that it the culprit. And from it as from an evil core that the what is the wrong word the evil spread. And none to urge—none to have urged its demolition. As if doomed to endure. Question answered. Chalkstones of striking effect in the light of the moon. Let it be in opposition when the skies are clear. Quick then still under the spell of Venus quick to the other window to see the other marvel rise. How whiter and whiter as it climbs it whitens more and more the stones. Rigid with face and hands against the pane she stands and marvels long.

The two zones form a roughly circular whole. As though out-lined by a trembling hand. Diameter. Care-ful. Say one furlong. On an average. Beyond the unknown. Mercifully. The feeling at times of being below sea level.

Especially at night when the skies are clear. Invisible nearby sea. Inaudible. The entire surface under grass. Once clear of the zone of stones. Save where it has receded from the chalky soil. Innumerable white scabs all shapes and sizes. Of striking effect in the light of the moon. In the way of animals ovines only. After long hesitation. They are white and make do with little. Whence suddenly come no knowing nor whither as suddenly gone. Unshepherded they stray as they list. Flowers? Careful. Alone the odd crocus still at lambing time. And man? Shut of at last? Alas no. For will she not be surprised one day to find him gone? Surprised no she is beyond surprise. How many? A figure come what may. Twelve. Wherewith to furnish the horizon's narrow round. She raises her eyes and sees one. Turns away and sees another. So on. Always afar. Still or receding. She never once saw one come toward her. Or she forgets. She forgets. Are they always the same? Do they see her? Enough.

A moor would have bet-
ter met the case. Were there a case better
to meet. There had to be lambs. Rightly or
wrongly. A moor would have allowed of
them. Lambs for their whiteness. And for
other reasons as yet obscure. Another reason. And so that there may be none. At
lambing time. That from one moment to
the next she may raise her eyes to find
them gone. A moor would have allowed of
them. In any case too late. And what
lambs. No trace of frolic. White splotches
in the grass. Aloof from the unheeding
ewes. Still. Then a moment straying. Then
still again. To think there is still life in this
age. Gently gently.

She is drawn to a certain
spot. At times. There stands a stone. It it is
draws her. Rounded rectangular block
three times as high as wide. Four. Her stature now. Her lowly stature. When it draws

she must to it. She cannot see it from her door. Blindfold she could find her way. With herself she has no more converse. Never had much. Now none. As had she the misfortune to be still of this world. But when the stone draws then to her feet the prayer, Take her. Especially at night when the skies are clear. With moon or without. They take her and halt her before it. There she too as if of stone. But black. Sometimes in the light of the moon. Mostly of the stars alone. Does she envy it?

To the imaginary stranger the dwelling appears deserted. Under constant watch it betrays no sign of life. The eye glued to one or the other window has nothing but black drapes for its pains. Motionless against the door he listens long. No sound. Knocks. No answer. Watches all night in vain for the least glimmer. Returns at last to his own and avows, No one. She shows herself only to her own. But she has no own. Yes yes she has one. And who has her.

There was a time when she did not appear in the zone of stones. A long time. Was not therefore to be seen going out or coming in. When she appeared only in the pastures. Was not therefore to be seen leaving them. Save as though by enchantment. But little by little she began to appear. In the zone of stones. First darkly. Then more and more plain. Till in detail she could be seen crossing the threshold both ways and closing the door behind her. Then a time when within her walls she did not appear. A long time. But little by little she began to appear. Within her walls. Darkly. Time truth to tell still current. Though she within them no more. This long time.

Yes within her walls so far at the window only. At one or the other window. Rapt before the sky. And only half seen so far a pallet and a ghostly chair. Ill half seen. And how in her faint comings and goings she suddenly stops dead. And how hard set to rise up from off her knees. But there too little by little she begins to appear more plain. Within her walls. As well as other objects. Such as under her pillow—such as deep in some recess this still shadowy album. Perhaps in time be by her when she takes it on her knees. See the old fingers fumble through the pages. And what scenes they can possibly be that draw the head down lower still and hold it in thrall. In the meantime who knows no more than withered flowers. No more!

But quick seize her where she is best to be seized. In the pastures far from shelter. She crosses the zone of stones and is there. Clearer and clearer as she goes. Quick seeing she goes out less and less. And so to say only in winter. Winter in her winter haunts she wanders. Far from shelter. Head bowed she makes her slow wavering way across the snow. It is evening. Yet again. On the snow her long shadow keeps her company. The others are there. All about. The twelve. Afar. Still or receding. She raises her eyes and sees one. Turns away and sees another. Again she stops dead. Now the moment or never. But something forbids. Just time to begin to glimpse a fringe of black veil. The face must wait. Just time before the eye cast down. Where nothing to be seen in the grazing rays but snow. And how all about little by little her footprints are effaced.

What is it defends her? Even from her own. Averts the intent gaze. Incriminates the dearly won. Forbids divining her. What but life ending. Hers. The other's. But so otherwise. She needs nothing. Nothing utterable. Whereas the other. How need in the end? But how? How need in the end?

Times when she is gone. Long lapses of time. At crocus time it would be making for the distant tomb. To have that on the imagination! On top of the rest. Bearing by the stem or round her arm the cross or wreath. But she can be gone at any time. From one moment of the year to the next suddenly no longer there. No longer anywhere to be seen. Nor by the eye of flesh nor by the other. Then as suddenly there again. Long after. So on. Any other would renounce. Avow, No one. No one more. Any other than this other. In wait for her to reappear. In order to resume. Resume the—what is the word? What the wrong word?

Riveted to some detail of the desert the eye fills with tears. Imagination at wit's end spreads its sad wings. Gone she hears one night the sea as if afar. Plucks up her long skirt to make better haste and discovers her boots and stockings to the calf. Tears. Last example the

flagstone before her door that by dint by
dint her little weight has grooved. Tears.

Before left for the stock-
ings the boots have time to be ill buttoned.
Weeping over as weeping will see now the
buttonhook larger than life. Of tarnished
silver pisciform it hangs by its hook from a
nail. It trembles faintly without cease. As
if here without cease the earth faintly
quaked. The oval handle is wrought to a
semblance of scales. The shank a little bent
leads up to the hook the eye so far still dry.
A lifetime of hooking has lessened its cur-
vature. To the point at certain moments of
its seeming unfit for service. Child's play
with a pliers to restore it. Was there once a
time she did? Careful. Once once in a way.
Till she could no more. No more bring the
jaws together. Oh not for weakness. Since
when it hangs useless from the nail. Trem-

bling imperceptibly without cease. Silver
shimmers some evenings when the skies
are clear. Close-up then. In which in de-
fiance of reason the nail prevails. Long this
image till suddenly it blurs.

She is there. Again. Let
the eye from its vigil be distracted a moment. At break or close of day. Distracted
by the sky. By something in the sky. So
that when it resumes the curtain may be
no longer closed. Opened by her to let
her see the sky. But even without that
she is there. Without the curtain's being
opened. Suddenly open. A flash. The sud-
denness of all! She still without stopping.
On her way without starting. Gone without going. Back without returning. Suddenly it is evening. Or dawn. The eye
rivets the bare window. Nothing in the
sky will distract it from it more. While she

from within looks her fill. Pfft occulted.
Nothing having stirred.

Already all confusion.
Things and imaginings. As of always. Confusion amounting to nothing. Despite precautions. If only she could be pure
figment. Unalloyed. This old so dying
woman. So dead. In the madhouse of the
skull and nowhere else. Where no more
precautions to be taken. No precautions
possible. Cooped up there with the rest.
Hovel and stones. The lot. And the eye.
How simple all then. If only all could be
pure figment. Neither be nor been nor by
any shift to be. Gently gently. On. Careful.

Here to the rescue two
lights. Two small skylights. Set in the

high-pitched roof on either side. Each
shedding dim light. No ceiling therefore.
Necessarily. Otherwise with the curtains
closed she would be in the dark. Day and
night in the dark. And what of it? She is
done with raising her eyes. Nearly done.
But when she lies with them open she can
just make out the rafters. In the dim light
the skylights shed. An ever dimmer light.
As the panes slowly dimmen. All in black
she comes and goes. The hem of her long
black skirt brushes the floor. But most
often she is still. Standing or sitting. Lying
or on her knees. In the dim light the skylights shed. Otherwise with the curtains
closed for preference she would be in the
dark. In the dark day and night.

Next to emerge from
the shadows an inner wall. Only slowly to
dissolve in favour of a single space. East the
bed. West the chair. A place divided by her

use of it alone. How more desirable in every way an interior of a piece. The eye breathes again but not for long. For slowly it emerges again. Rises from the floor and slowly up to lose itself in the gloom. The semigloom. It is evening. The button-hook glimmers in the last rays. The pallet scarce to be seen.

Weary of the inanimate the eye in her absence falls back on the twelve. Out of her sight as she of theirs. Alone turn where she may she keeps her eyes fixed on the ground. On the way at her feet where it has come to a stop. Winter evening. Not to be precise. All so bygone. To the twelve then for want of better the widowed eye. No matter which. In the distance stiff he stands facing front and the setting sun. Dark greatcoat reaching to the ground. Antiquated block hat. Finally the face caught full in the last rays.

Quick enlarge and devour before night falls.

Having no need of light to see the eye makes haste. Before night falls. So it is. So itself belies. Then glutted—then torpid under its lid makes way for unreason. What if not her do they ring around? Careful. She who looks up no more looks up and sees them. Some among them. Still or receding. Receding. Those too closely seen who move to preserve their distance. While at the same time others advance. Those in the wake of her wandering. She never once saw one come toward her. Or she forgets. She forgets. Now some do. Toward but never nearer. Thus they keep her in the centre. More or less. What then if not her do they ring around? In their ring whence she disappears unhindered. Whence they let her disappear. Instead of disappearing in her company. So the unreasoning goes. While the eye digests its pittance. In its private dark. In the general dark.

As hope expires of her ever reappearing she reappears. At first sight little changed. It is evening. It will always be evening. When not night. She emerges at the fringe of the pastures and sets forward across them. Slowly with fluttering step as if wanting mass. Suddenly still and as suddenly on her way again. At this rate it will be black night before she reaches home. Home! But time slows all this while. Suits its speed to hers. Whence from beginning to end of her course no loss or but little of twilight. A matter at most of a candle or two. Bearing south as best she can she casts toward the moon to come her long black shadow. They come at last to the door holding a great key. At the same instant night. When not evening night. Head bowed she stands exposed facing east. All dead still. All save hanging from a finger the old key polished by use. Trembling it faintly shimmers in the light of the moon.

Wooed from below the face consents at last. In the dim light reflected by the flag. Calm slab worn and polished by agelong comings and goings. Livid pallor. Not a wrinkle. How serene it seems this ancient mask. Worthy those worn by certain newly dead. True the light leaves to be desired. The lids occult the longed-for eyes. Time will tell them washen blue. Where tears perhaps not for nothing. Unimaginable tears of old. Lashes jet black remains of the brunette she was. Perhaps once was. When yet a lass. Yet brunette. Skipping the nose at the call of the lips these no sooner broached are withdrawn. The slab having darkened with the darkening sky. Black night henceforward. And at dawn an empty place. With no means of knowing whether she has gone in or under cover of darkness her ways again.

White stones more plentiful every year. As well say every instant. In a fair way if they persist to bury all. First zone rather more extensive than at first sight ill seen and every year rather more. Of striking effect in the light of the moon these millions of little sepulchres. But in her absence but cold comfort. From it then in the end to the second miscalled pastures. Leprous with white scars where the grass has receded from the chalky soil. In contemplation of this erosion the eye finds solace. Everywhere stone is gaining. Whiteness. More and more every year. As well say every instant. Everywhere every instant whiteness is gaining.

The eye will return to the scene of its betrayals. On centennial leave from where tears freeze. Free again an instant to shed them scalding. On the blest tears once shed. While exulting at the white heap of stone. Ever heaping for want of better on itself. Which if it persist will gain the skies. The moon. Venus.

From the stones she steps down into the pastures. As from one tier of a circus to the next. A gap time will fill. For faster than the stones invade it the other ground upheaves its own. So far in silence. A silence time will break. This great silence evening and night. Then all along the verge the muffled thud of stone on stone. Of those spilling their excess on those emergent. Only now and then at first. Then at ever briefer intervals. Till one continuous din. With none to hear. Decreasing as the levels draw together to silence once again. Evening and night. In the meantime she is suddenly sitting with her feet in the pastures. Were it not for the empty hands on the way who knows to the tomb. Back from it then more likely. On the way back from the tomb. Frozen true to her wont she seems turned to stone. Face to the further confines the eye closes in vain to see. At last they appear an instant. North where she passes them always. Shroud of radiant haze. Where to melt into paradise.

The long white hair stares in a fan. Above and about the impassive face. Stares as if shocked still by some ancient horror. Or by its continuance. Or by another. That leaves the face stone-cold. Silence at the eye of the scream. Which say? Ill say. Both. All three. Question answered.

Seated on the stones she is seen from behind. From the waist up. Trunk black rectangle. Nape under frill of black lace. White half halo of hair. Face to the north. The tomb. Eyes on the horizon perhaps. Or closed to see the headstone. The withered crocuses. Endless evening. She lit aslant by the last rays. They make no difference. None to the black of the cloth. None to the white hair. It too dead still. In the still air. Voidlike calm as always. Evening and night. Suffice to watch the grass. How motionless it droops. Till under the relentless eye it shivers. With faintest shiver from its innermost. Equally the hair. Rigidly horrent it shivers at last for the eye about to abandon. And the old body itself. When it seems of stone. Is it not in fact ashiver from head to foot? Let her but go and stand still by the other stone. It white from afar in the pastures. And the eye go from one to the other. Back and forth. What calm then. And what storm. Beneath the weeds' mock calm.

Not possible any longer except as figment. Not endurable. Nothing for it but to close the eye for good and see her. Her and the rest. Close it for good and all and see her to death. Unremittent. In the shack. Over the stones. In the pastures. The haze. At the tomb. And back. And the rest. For good and all. To death. Be shut of it all. On to the next. Next figment. Close it for good this filthy eye of flesh. What forbids? Careful.

Such—such fiasco that folly takes a hand. Such bits and scraps. Seen no matter how and said as seen. Dread of black. Of white. Of void. Let her vanish. And the rest. For good. And the sun. Last rays. And the moon. And Venus. Nothing left but black sky. White earth. Or inversely. No more sky or earth. Finished high and low. Nothing but black and white. Everywhere no matter where. But black. Void. Nothing else. Contemplate that. Not another word. Home at last. Gently gently.

Panic past pass on. The hands. Seen from above. They rest on the pubis intertwined. Strident white. Their faintly leaden tinge killed by the black ground. Suspicion of lace at the wrists. To go with the frill. They tighten then loosen their clasp. Slow systole diastole. And the body that scandal. While its sole hands in view. On its sole pubis. Dead still to be sure. On the chair. After the spectacle. Slowly its spell unbinding. On and on they keep. Tightening and loosening their clasp. Rhythm of a labouring heart. Till when almost despaired of gently part. Suddenly gently. Spreading rise and in midair palms uppermost come to rest. Behold our hollows. Then after a moment as if to hide the lines fall back pronating as they go and light flat on head of thighs. Within an ace of the crotch. It is now the left hand lacks its third finger. A swelling no doubt—a swelling no doubt of the knuckle between first and second phalanges preventing one panic day withdrawal of the ring. The kind called keeper. Still as stones they defy as stones do the eye. Do they as much as feel the clad flesh? Does the clad flesh feel them? Will they then never quiver? This night assuredly not. For before they have—before the eye has time they mist. Who is to blame? Or what? They? The eye? The missing finger? The keeper? The cry?

What cry? All five. All six. And the rest. All. All to blame. All.

Winter evening in the pastures. The snow has ceased. Her steps so light they barely leave a trace. Have barely left having ceased. Just enough to be still visible. Adrift the snow. Whither in her head while her feet stray thus? Hither and thither too? Or unswerving to the mirage? And where when she halts? The eye discerns afar a kind of stain. Finally the steep roof whence part of the fresh fall has slid. Under the low lowering sky the north is lost. Obliterated by the snow the twelve are there. Invisible were she to raise her eyes. She on the contrary immaculately black. Not having received a single flake. Nothing needed now but for them to start falling again which therefore they do. First one by one here and there. Then thicker

and thicker plumb through the still air.
Slowly she disappears. Together with the
trace of her steps and that of the distant
roof. How find her way home? Home!
Even as the homing bird. Safe as the saying
is and sound.

All dark in the cabin
while she whitens afar. Silence but for the
imaginary murmur of flakes beating on the
roof. And every now and then a real creak.
Her company. Here without having to
close the eye sees her afar. Motionless in
the snow under the snow. The buttonhook trembles from its nail as if a night
like any other. Facing the black curtain the
chair exudes its solitude. For want of a fel-
low-table. Far from it in a corner see suddenly an antique coffer. In its therefore no
lesser solitude. It perhaps that creaks. And
in its depths who knows the key. The key

to close. But this night the chair. Its immovable air. Less than the—more than the empty seat the barred back is piteous. Here if she eats here she sits to eat. The eye closes in the dark and sees her in the end. With her right hand as large as life she holds the edge of the bowl resting on her knees. With her left the spoon dipped in the slop. She waits. For it to cool perhaps. But no. Merely frozen again just as about to begin. At last in a twin movement full of grace she slowly raises the bowl toward her lips while at the same time with equal slowness bowing her head to join it. Having set out at the same instant they meet halfway and there come to rest. Fresh rigor before the first spoonful slobbered largely back into the slop. Others no happier till time to part lips and bowl and slowly back with never a slip to their starting points. As smooth and even fro as to. Now again the rigid Memnon pose. With her right hand she holds the edge of the bowl. With her left the spoon dipped in the slop. So far so good. But before she can proceed she fades and disappears. Nothing now for the staring eye but the chair in its solitude.

One evening she was followed by a lamb. Reared for slaughter like the others it left them to follow her. In the present to conclude. All so bygone. Slaughter apart it is not like the others. Hanging to the ground in matted coils its fleece hides the little shanks. Rather than walk it seems to glide like a toy in tow. It halts at the same instant as she. At the same instant as she strays on. Stockstill as she it waits with head like hers extravagantly bowed. Clash of black and white that far from muting the last rays amplify. It is now her puniness leaps to the eye. Thanks it would seem to the lowly creature next her. Brief paradox. For suddenly together they move on. Hither and thither toward the stones. There she turns and sits.

Does she see the white body at her feet?
Head haught now she gazes into empti-
ness. That profusion. Or with closed eyes
sees the tomb. The lamb goes no further.
Alone night fallen she makes for home.
Home! As straight as were it to be seen.

Was it ever over and
done with questions? Dead the whole
brood no sooner hatched. Long before. In
the egg. Long before. Over and done with
answering. With not being able. With not
being able not to want to know. With not
being able. No. Never. A dream. Question
answered.

What remains for the
eye exposed to such conditions? To such
vicissitude of hardly there and wholly

gone. Why none but to open no more. Till all done. She done. Or left undone. Tenement and unreason. No more unless to rest. In the outward and so-called visible. That daub. Quick again to the brim the old nausea and shut again. On her. Till she be whole. Or abort. Question answered.

The coffer. Empty after long nocturnal search. Nothing. Save in the end in a cranny of dust a scrap of paper. Jagged along one edge as if torn from a diary. On its yellowed face in barely legible ink two letters followed by a number. Tu 17. Or Th. Tu or Th 17. Otherwise blank. Otherwise empty.

She reemerges on her back. Dead still. Evening and night. Dead still

on her back evening and night. The bed.
Careful. A pallet? Hardly if head as ill seen
when on her knees. Praying if she prays.
Pah she has only to grovel deeper. Or
grovel elsewhere. Before the chair. Or the
coffer. Or at the edge of the pastures with
her head on the stones. A pallet then flat
on the floor. No pillow. Hidden from chin
to foot under a black covering she offers
her face alone. Alone! Face defenceless evening and night. Quick the eyes. The moment they open. Suddenly they are there.
Nothing having stirred. One is enough.
One staring eye. Gaping pupil thinly nim-
bed with washen blue. No trace of hu-
mour. None any more. Unseeing. As if
dazed by what seen behind the lids. The
other plumbs its dark. Then opens in its
turn. Dazed in its turn.

Incontinent the void. The
zenith. Evening again. When not night it

will be evening. Death again of deathless day. On the one hand embers. On the other ashes. Day without end won and lost. Unseen.

On resumption the head is covered. No matter. No matter now. Such the confusion now between real and—how say its contrary? No matter. That old tandem. Such now the confusion between them once so twain. And such the farrago from eye to mind. For it to make what sad sense of it may. No matter now. Such equal liars both. Real and—how ill say its contrary? The counter-poison.

Still fresh the coffer fiasco what now of all things but a trapdoor. So cunningly contrived that even to the lidded eye it scarcely shows. Careful. Raise it at once and risk another rebuff? No question. Simply savour in advance with in mind the grisly cupboard its conceivable contents. For the first time then wooden floor. Its boards in line with the trap's designed to conceal it. Promising this flagrant concern with camouflage. But beware. Question by the way what wood of all woods? Ebony why not? Ebony boards. Black on black the brushing skirt. Stark the skeleton chair death-paler than life.

While head included she lies hidden time for a turn in the pastures. No shock were she already dead. As of course she is. But in the meantime more convenient not. Still living then she lies hidden. Having for some reason covered her head. Or for no reason. Night. When not evening night. Winter night. No snow. For the sake of variety. To vary the monotony. The limp grass strangely rigid under the weight of the rime. Clawed by the long black skirt how if but heard it must murmur. Moonless star-studded sky reflected in the erosions filmed with ice. The silence merges into music infinitely far and as unbroken as silence. Ceaseless celestial winds in unison. For all all matters now. The stones gleam faintly afar and the cabin walls seen white at last. Said white. The guardians—the twelve are there but not at full muster. Well! Above all not understand. Simply note how those still faithful have moved apart. Such ill seen that night in the pastures. While head included she lies hidden. Under on closer inspection a long greatcoat. A man's by the buttons. The buttonholes. Eyes closed does she see him?

White walls. High time. White as new. No wind. Not a breath.

Unbeaten on by all that comes beating
down. And mystery the sun has spared
them. The sun that once beat down. So
east and west sides the required clash.
South gable no problem. But the other.
That door. Careful. Black too? Black too.
And the roof. Slates. More. Small slates
black too brought from a ruined mansion.
What tales had they tongues to tell. Their
long tale told. Such the dwelling ill seen ill
said. Outwardly. High time.

Changed the stone that
draws her when revisited alone. Or she
who changes it when side by side. Now
alone it leans. Backward or forward as the
case may be. Is it to nature alone it owes its
rough-hewn air? Or to some too human
hand forced to desist? As Michelangelo's
from the regicide's bust. If there may not
be no more questions let there at least be
no more answers. Granite of no common

variety assuredly. Black as jade the jasper that flecks its whiteness. On its what is the wrong word its uptilted face obscure graffiti. Scrawled by the ages for the eye to solicit in vain. Winter evenings on her doorstep she imagines she can see it glitter afar. When from their source in the west-south-west the last rays rake its averse face. Such ill seen the stone alone where it stands at the far fringe of the pastures. On her way out with the flowers as unerring as best she can she lingers by it. As on her way back with empty hands. Lingers by it a while on her way on. Toward the one or other abode. As unerring as best she can.

See them again side by side. Not quite touching. Lit aslant by the latest last rays they cast to the east-north-east their long parallel shadows. Evening therefore. Winter evening. It will always be evening. Always winter. When not night. Winter night. No more lambs. No more flowers. Empty-handed she shall go to the tomb. Until she go no more. Or no more return. So much for that. Undistinguishable the twin shadows. Till one at length more dense as if of a body better opaque. At length more still. As faintly at length the other trembles under the staring gaze. Throughout this confrontation the sun stands still. That is to say the earth. Not to recoil on until the parting. Then on its face over the pastures and then the stones the still living shadow slowly glides. Lengthening and fading more and more. But never quite away. Under the hovering eye.

Close-up of a dial. Nothing else. White disc divided in minutes. Unless it be in seconds. Sixty black dots.

No figure. One hand only. Finest of fine black darts. It advances by fits and starts. No tick. Leaps from dot to dot with so lightning a leap that but for its new position it had not stirred. Whole nights may pass as may but a fraction of a second or any intermediate lapse of time soever before it flings itself from one degree to the next. None at any moment overleaping in all fairness be it said. Let it when discovered be pointing east. Having thus covered after its fashion assuming the instrument plumb the first quarter of its latest hour. Unless it be its latest minute. Then doubt certain—then despair certain nights of its ever attaining the last. Ever regaining north.

She reappears at evening at her window. When not night evening. If she will see Venus again she must open it. Well! First draw aside the curtain and then open. Head bowed she waits to be able. Mindful perhaps of evenings when she was able too late. Black night fallen. But no. In her head too pure wait. The curtain. Seen closer thanks to this hiatus it reveals itself at last for what it is. A black greatcoat. Hooked by its tails from the rod it hangs sprawling inside out like a carcass in a butcher's stall. Or better inside in for the pathos of the dangling arms. Same infinitesimal quaver as the buttonhook and passim. Another novelty the chair drawn up to the window. This to raise the line of sight on the fair prey loftier when first sighted than at first sight ill seen. What empty space henceforward. For long pacing to and fro in the gloom. Suddenly in a single gesture she snatches aside the coat and to again on a sky as black as it. And then? Careful. Have her sit? Lie? Kneel? Go? She too vacillates. Till in the end the back and forth prevails. Sends her wavering north and south from wall to wall. In the kindly dark.

She is vanishing. With the rest. The already ill seen bedimmed and ill seen again annulled. The mind betrays the treacherous eyes and the treacherous word their treacheries. Haze sole certitude. The same that reigns beyond the pastures. It gains them already. It will gain the zone of stones. Then the dwelling through all its chinks. The eye will close in vain. To see but haze. Not even. Be itself but haze. How can it ever be said? Quick how ever ill said before it submerges all. Light. In one treacherous word. Dazzling haze. Light in its might at last. Where no more to be seen. To be said. Gently gently.

The face yet again in the light of the last rays. No loss of pallor. None of cold. Suspended on the verge for this sight the westering sun. That is the eastering earth. The thin lips seem as if never again to part. Peeping from their join a suspicion of pulp. Unlikely site of olden kisses given and received. Or given only. Or received only. Impressive above all the corners imperceptibly upcurved. A smile? Is it possible? Ghost of an ancient smile smiled finally once and for all. Such ill half seen the mouth in the light of the last rays. Suddenly they leave it. Rather it leaves them. Off again to the dark. There to smile on. If smile is what it is.

Reexamined rid of light the mouth changes. Unexplainably. Lips as before. Same closure. Same hint of extruding pulp. At the corners same imperceptible laxness. In a word the smile still there if smile is what it is. Neither more nor less. Less! And yet no longer the same. True that light distorts. Particularly sunset. That mockery. True too that the eyes then agaze for the viewless planet are now closed. On other viewlessness. Of which more if ever anon. There the explanation at last. This same smile established with eyes open is with them closed no longer the same. Though between the two inspections the mouth unchanged. Utterly. Good. But in what way no longer the same? What there now that was not there? What there no more that was? Enough. Away.

Back after many winters. Long after in this endless winter. This endless heart of winter. Too soon. She as when fled. Where as when fled. Still or again. Eyes closed in the dark. To the dark. In their own dark. On the lips same minute smile. If smile is what it is. In short alive as she alone knows how neither more nor less. Less! Compared to true stone. Within as sadly as before all as at first sight ill seen.

With the happy exception of the lights'
enhanced opacity. Dim the light of day
from them were day again to dawn. Without on the other hand some progress.
Toward unbroken night. Universal stone.
Day no sooner risen fallen. Scrapped all the
ill seen ill said. The eye has changed. And
its drivelling scribe. Absence has changed
them. Not enough. Time to go again.
Where still more to change. Whence back
too soon. Changed but not enough.
Strangers but not enough. To all the ill
seen ill said. Then back again. Disarmed for
to finish with it all at last. With her and her
rags of sky and earth. And if again too soon
go again. Change still more again. Then
back again. Barring impediment. Ah. So
on. Till fit to finish with it all at last. All the
trash. In unbroken night. Universal stone.
So first go. But first see her again. As when
fled. And the abode. That under the
changed eye it too may change. Begin. Just
one parting look. Before all meet again.
Then go. Barring impediment. Ah.

But see she suddenly no longer there. Where suddenly fled. Quick then the chair before she reappears. At length. Every angle. With what one word convey its change? Careful. Less. Ah the sweet one word. Less. It is less. The same but less. Whencesoever the glare. True that the light. See now how words too. A few drops mishaphazard. Then strangury. To say the least. Less. It will end by being no more. By never having been. Divine prospect. True that the light.

Suddenly enough and way for remembrance. Closed again to that end the vile jelly or opened again or left as it was however that was. Till all recalled. First finally by far hanging from their skirts two black greatcoats. Followed by the first hazy outlines of what possibly a hutch when suddenly enough. Remembrance! When all worse there than when first ill seen. The pallet. The chair. The coffer. The trap. Alone the eye has changed. Alone can cause to change. In the meantime nothing wanting. Wrong. The buttonhook. The nail. Wrong. There they are again. Still. Worse there than ever. Unchanged for the worse. Ope eye and at them to begin. But first the partition. It rid they too would be. It less they by as much.

It of all the properties doubtless the least obdurate. See the instant see it again when unaided it dissolved. So to say of itself. With no help from the eye. Not till long after to reappear. As if reluctantly. For what reason? For one not far to seek. For others then said obscure. One other above all. One other still far to seek. Analogy of the heart?

The skull? Hear from here the howls of laughter of the damned.

Enough. Quicker. Quick see how all in keeping with the chair. Minimally less. No more. Well on the way to inexistence. As to zero the infinite. Quick say. And of her? As much. Quick find her again. In that black heart. That mock brain.

The sheet. Between tips of trembling fingers. In two. Four. Eight. Old frantic fingers. Not paper any more. Each eighth apart. In two. Four. Finish with the knife. Hack into shreds. Down the plughole. On to the next. White. Quick blacken.

Alone the face remains. Of the rest beneath its covering no trace. During the inspection a sudden sound. Startling without consequence for the gaze the mind awake. How explain it? And without going so far how say it? Far behind the eye the quest begins. What time the event recedes. When suddenly to the rescue it comes again. Forthwith the uncommon common noun collapsion. Reinforced a little later if not enfeebled by the infrequent slumberous. A slumberous collapsion. Two. Then far from the still agonizing eye a gleam of hope. By the grace of these modest beginnings. With in second sight the shack in ruins. To scrute together with the inscrutable face. All curiosity spent.

Later while the face still unyielding another sound of fall but this time sharp. Heightening the fond illusion of general havoc in train. Here a great leap into what brief future remains and summary puncture of that puny balloon. Far ahead to the instant when the coats will have gone from their rods and the buttonhook from its nail. And been hove the sigh no more than that. Sigh upon sigh till all sighed quite away. All the fond trash. Destined before being to be no more than that. Last sighs. Of relief.

Quick beforehand again two mysteries. Not even. Mild shocks. Not even. In such abeyance the mind then. And from then on. First the curtains gone without loss of dark. Sweet foretaste of the joy at journey's end. Second after long hesitation no trace of the fallen where they fell. No trace of all the ado. Alone on the one hand the rods alone. A little bent. And alone on the other most alone the nail. Unimpaired. All set to serve again. Like unto its glorious ancestors. At the place of the skull. One April afternoon. Deposition done.

Full glare now on the face present throughout the recent future. As seen ill seen throughout the past neither more nor less. Less! Collated with its cast it lives beyond a doubt. Were it only by virtue of its imperfect pallor. And imperceptible tremor unworthy of true plaster. Heartening on the other hand the eyes persistently closed. No doubt a record in this position. Unobserved at least till now. Suddenly the look. Nothing having stirred. Look? Too weak a word. Too wrong. Its absence? No better. Unspeakable globe. Unbearable.

Ample time none the less a few seconds for the iris to be lacking.

Wholly. As if engulfed by the pupil. And for the sclerotic not to say the white to appear reduced by half. Already that much less at least but at what cost. Soon to be foreseen save unforeseen two black blanks. Fit ventholes of the soul that jakes. Here reappearance of the skylights opaque to no purpose henceforward. Seeing the black night or better blackness pure and simple that limpid they would shed. Blackness in its might at last. Where no more to be seen. Perforce to be seen.

Absence supreme good and yet. Illumination then go again and on return no more trace. On earth's face. Of what was never. And if by mishap some left then go again. For good again. So on. Till no more trace. On earth's face. Instead of always the same place. Slaving away forever in the same place. At this and that trace. And what if the eye could not? No more tear itself away from the remains of trace. Of what was never. Quick say it suddenly can and farewell say say farewell. If only to the face. Of her tenacious trace.

Decision no sooner reached or rather long after than what is the wrong word? For the last time at last for to end yet again what the wrong word? Than revoked. No but slowly dispelled a little very little like the last wisps of day when the curtain closes. Of itself by slow millimetres or drawn by a phantom hand. Farewell to farewell. Then in that perfect dark foreknell darling sound pip for end begun. First last moment. Grant only enough remain to devour all. Moment by glutton moment. Sky earth the whole kit and boodle. Not another crumb of carrion left. Lick chops and basta. No. One moment more. One last. Grace to breathe that void. Know happiness.

OTHER WORKS BY SAMUEL BECKETT
PUBLISHED BY GROVE PRESS

Cascando and Other Short Dramatic Pieces (Words and Music; Eh Joe; Come and Go; Film [original version])

Collected Poems in English and French

The Collected Works of Samuel Beckett (twenty-four volumes)

Company

Endgame

Ends and Odds (Not I; That Time; Footfalls; Ghost Trio; . . .but the clouds . . .; Theatre I; Theatre II; Radio I; Radio II)

Film, A Film Script

First Love and Other Shorts (From an Abandoned Work; Enough; Imagination Dead Imagine; Ping; Not I; Breath)

Fizzles

Happy Days

How It Is

I Can't Go On, I'll Go On: A Selection from Samuel Beckett's Work

Krapp's Last Tape and Other Dramatic Pieces (All That Fall [radio]; Embers [radio]; Acts Without Words I and II [mimes])

The Lost Ones

Malone Dies